I0608248

Saturday Popular Concerts.

———

Director—Mr. S. ARTHUR CHAPPELL.

Four Hundred and Eighty-seventh Concert.*

PROGRAMME FROM THE WORKS OF

Various Masters.

SATURDAY AFTERNOON, NOVEMBER 14th, 1874.

QUARTET, in G major, Op. 54, No. 2, for two Violins,
Viola, and Violoncello.   *Haydn.*

(First performance at the Popular Concerts.)

Allegro con brio—G major.
Allegretto—C major.
Minuetto and Trio—G major.
Presto (Finale)—G major.

M. SAINTON, Herr L. RIES, Mr. ZERBINI,
and Signor PEZZE.

Nothing more purely and legitimately Haydn than this
quartet exists in its composer's almost inexhaustible repertory.

Second Concert of the Seventeenth Season.

The *allegro con brio* sets out with the following spirited and well-developed theme:—

The foregoing is cited at unusual length, because, with the exception of an occasional episode, as attentive hearers will not fail to observe, it forms the *substratum* of the entire movement. Here, for example, is an episode in question :—

This half close brings back the leading theme in the original key; but, as will be seen below, it soon gives way to a counter theme, in the orthodox dominant :—

The further development of this second subject is made noticeable by the introduction of a prominent feature in the leading theme (☞) :—

After a full close in D, comes the peroration, in which, as will be observed, the same phrase (☞) again plays a conspicuous part :—

The foregoing materials are all made use of in the second division of the *allegro*, which, like the first, is meant to be repeated. The elaborate development of this "free *fantasia*" must, however, speak for itself. The movement comes to an end with a reference to the leading theme, beginning on an interrupted cadence (*), and twice more invaded by the particular phrase which has already been thrice referred to (𝄢) :—

Haydn himself has written no more homogeneous movement than this *allegro con brio*.

Allegretto (theme).

Further quotation from so unpretending and simply constructed a movement would be superfluous.

54

Minuetto.

Trio.

1st Violin *tacet.*

Presto (leading theme).

(Episode—G minor.)

This movement is in the *rondo* form. The theme re-appears several times, and each time in a modified shape as regards all except the melody, short episodes always pre-

K

paring the *rentreé.* A brilliant *coda,* for the four instruments in unison, introduces us to a last glimpse of the theme, on a dominant pedal :—

One of the gayest and freshest of its nearly always cheerful composer's movements of the kind, and sparkling with quiet humour, it can never fail to impress and charm.

LIEDER, Miss ANTOINETTE STERLING.

DER TOD UND DAS MÄDCHEN.   *Schubert.*

DAS MÄDCHEN.   Vorüber, ach! vorüber,
          Geh', wilder Knochenmann!
      Ich bin noch jung; geh', Lieber,
          Und rühre mich nicht an.

DER TOD.   Gieb deine Hand, du schön und zart Gebild;
          Bin Freund, und komme nicht zu strafen.
      Sei gutes Muths! ich bin nicht wild;
          Sollst sanft in meinen Armen schlafen.

"O JUGEND, O SCHÖNE ROSENZEIT."   *Mendelssohn.*

Von allen schönen Kindern auf der Welt
Mir eines doch am meisten wohlgefällt;
Est hat ein roth Mündlein, und dunkelbraunes Haar;
Wohl will ich es lieben auch ganz und gar.

Die Grübchen in den Wangen, das Grübchen in dem Kinn,
D'rin war mir gleich gefangen mein ganzer leichter Sinn,
Und in die blauen Augen, seh' ich da recht hinein,
Do möcht ich mein Lebtag gefangen d'rin sein!

O Jugend, o schöne Rosenzeit!
Die Wiege, die Stege, sind mit Blumen bestreut,
Der Himmel steht offen, man schaut die Engelein.
O könnt' ich, Herzliebchen, stets bei dir sein!

"O, SPRINGTIME OF YOUTH."

Of all the lovely children earth can shew,
There's one that pleases me the best, I trow;
Her lips are like rosebuds, and dark brown is her hair,
And all my love truly shall dwell with her.

Within her cheeks two dimples, and one upon her chin,
Securely lay a pris'ner my light heart soon therein;
And in her pretty blue eyes, if I look in them well,
I would all my days as a slave therein dwell!

O, springtime of youth, and rosy hours!
Thy ways are strew'd over with the fairest of flow'rs;
The Heavens are open, the Angels all we see.
O, were I, fair maiden, for e'er with thee!

———

ITALIAN CONCERTO, in F major, for Pianoforte alone.

J. S. Bach.

(Second performance at the Popular Concerts.)

Allegro animato—F major.
Andante molto espressivo—D minor.
Presto giojoso—F major.

Dr. HANS VON BÜLOW.

The name by which this work is generally recognized—
" *Italiänisches Concert* "— is probably derived from some
tradition of which it is impossible in the present day to learn
the origin. Kuhnau, Bach's contemporary, entitled it simply
" *Klavier-Sonate* " (sonata for the clavier). It is in three
movements; and here ends its affinity with those sonatas of
the great masters which are based upon the now universally
accepted plan that Haydn was the first to develop, and even
Beethoven, in his most extended compositions, has never
discarded. Bach's plan, according to this model, is no plan
at all. Each movement, nevertheless, is carried on with a
fluency that atones for the absence of what modern musicians
are taught to recognise as design. The *allegro* begins with
the subjoined vigorous phrase (mark the E flat at the end of
the third bar):—

The four bars are then repeated a fifth higher:—

The continuation is in the same vein:—

We are then brought to a sort of dominant episode, commencing thus:—

—and ultimately leading to a full close in the tonic (F), the temporary interruption of which (at the second bar *) is quite a modern effect:—

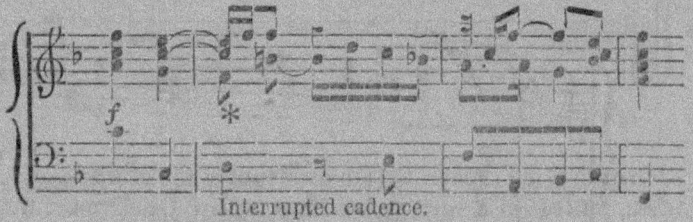

Interrupted cadence.

Now follows a phrase which the provoking E flat (*) prevents us at the outset from feeling to be openly and unconditionally in F :—

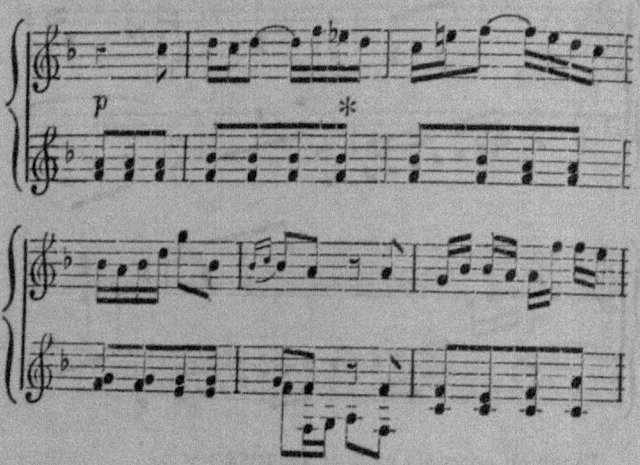

The foregoing, which may be regarded as the second subject, has some kind of resemblance to the phraseology of Domenico Scarlatti. Its development, in the course of which occurs the subjoined beautiful sequence :—

—leads to a full close in C (the dominant of the primary key), when, instead of a melody, we have a new treatment of the leading theme, divided again into two sections of two keys each—in the first, C and F; in the last, F and B flat:—

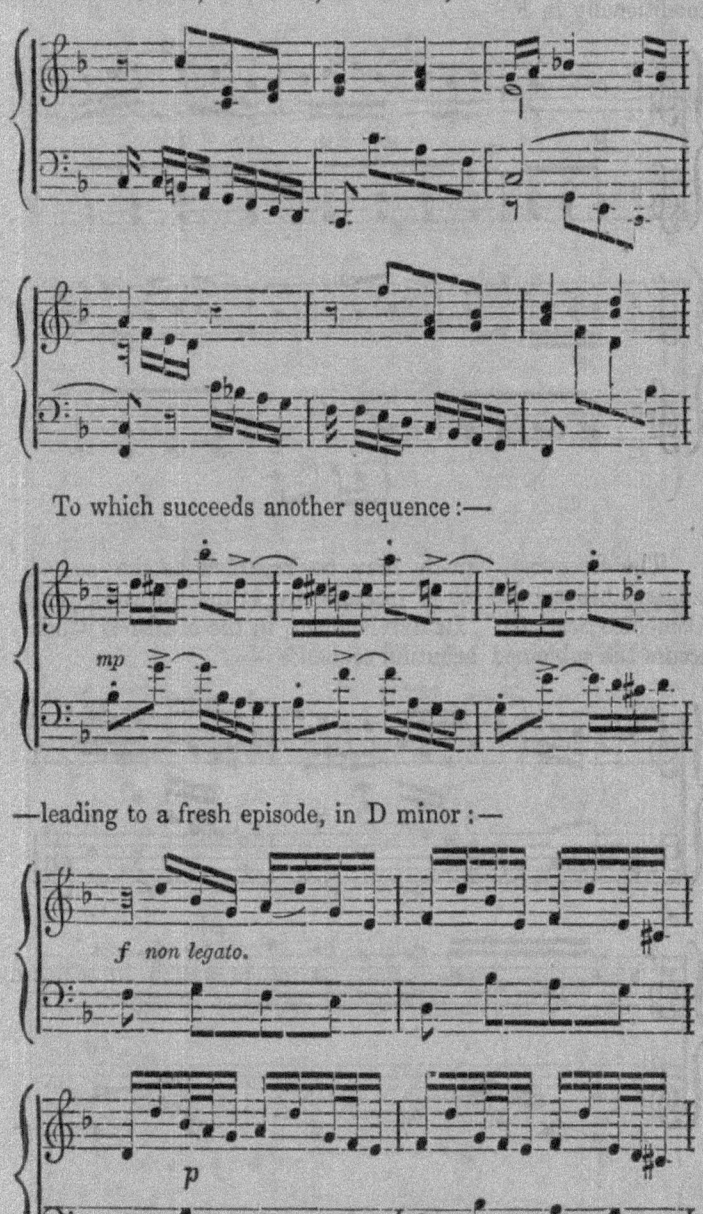

To which succeeds another sequence:—

—leading to a fresh episode, in D minor:—

—in which key we have a recurrence to the dominant episode :—

—and to the full close, with the interruption at the second bar :—

After a prolongation of the D minor section, in which a new phrase is introduced:—

—a passage in sequence, commencing thus :—

—leads to the key of B flat major, the principal subject now reappearing, and being carried on in a wholly new manner :—

A somewhat extended development of the foregoing (with further sequences) ultimately subsides on the dominant of F, in which primary key we are introduced to another new subject :—

64

In the progress of this we have a fresh allusion to the
leading theme :—

—a reference to the phrase in D minor (now in a major
key), already mentioned :—

—and further sequences, leading back to the original
theme :—

—thirty bars of which, up to the first full close, are repeated
notatim. And so this animated *allegro*—which has little
of the contrapuntal devices usually to be met with in the
compositions of J. S. Bach—comes to an end.

The slow movement, consisting of a lengthy, elaborate,

and ingenious development of a theme, the character of which
may be indicated by the subjoined extract :—

—is far more congenial to Bach, and far more like his way of
composing, than any part of the preceding *allegro*. In its
way it is a masterpiece.

The *finale* sets out with the following spirited subject :—

This *presto* is no more in the regular form of the Haydn first-movement than either of its precursors. It is therefore unnecessary (as it would be unprofitable) to attempt any description of its plan. The first full close in F (the primary) is immediately followed by another subject in the same key, an interesting example of free double counterpoint :—

After a progression into the dominant (C), the passage of double counterpoint is repeated in that key, and followed by a repetition of the principal theme, alike transposed. The full close in C is then followed by a new theme, or episode, half in F and half in B flat, according to what seems to be a strict rule in the concerto :—

When the foregoing materials have been further developed, through various keys, without any conspicuously apparent plan, the leading theme being introduced in A minor, with the subjoined preamble :—

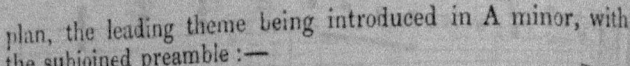

—the primary key of F major is regained; the first subject comes back in an unexpected manner; and, at the end of a couple of bars, is responded to by the episode already mentioned :—

When this is wrought out, we have a repetition of the theme in double counterpoint, somewhat more freely treated, and considerably modified in its development. A dominant pedal point of remarkable interest, begining thus:—

—then brings us back once more to the leading theme; and, as in the instance of the first movement, the *presto* terminates with a repetition, *notatim*, of a portion of the opening:—

Compared with the sonatas of Mozart and Beethoven, in which the form first developed by Haydn is carried out to its fullest perfection, or even to those of Dussek, Hummel, and others who have more or less successfully followed in their footsteps, this work of the great John Sebastian Bach may appear somewhat vague and unsymmetrical. Nevertheless, as it was avowedly an imitation, and therefore not strictly in his own incomparable style, he must not be judged by it. It should rather, indeed (or rather its first and last movements), be regarded as a *jeu d'esprit* on the part of the most earnest and profound of all composers.

The Italian Concerto was first introduced by Herr Ernst Pauer, at the twenty-first concert of the fourth season—May 19, 1862.

. Dr. HANS VON BÜLOW will perform on one of Messrs. JOHN BROADWOOD and SONS' Concert Grand Pianofortes.

SATURDAY POPULAR CONCERTS, ST. JAMES'S HALL.— On Saturday next, November 21, the Programme will include Beethoven's Quartet in F major, Op. 59, No. 1, for Strings ; Suite in F major, by J. S. Bach, for Pianoforte alone ; and Raff's Quintet in A minor, Op. 107, for Pianoforte and Strings (First time). Executants, MM. HANS VON BÜLOW, STRAUS, L. RIES, ZERBINI, and PIATTI. Vocalist, Mlle. NITA GAËTANO. Conductor, Sir JULIUS BENEDICT. To commence at Three o'Clock.

Sofa Stalls, 5s. Balcony, 3s. Admission, 1s. Tickets and Programmes at CHAPPELL & CO.'s, 50, New Bond Street.

Entr' Acte.

SIR JULIUS BENEDICT.

(From the " Daily Telegraph.")

There is no doubt that the business of giving testimonials has been carried to an extreme of late years, and should the indiscriminate pursuit of it go on much longer, men will be distinguished in an inverse ratio to the number they have received, the highest honour being his who has received none at all. But a good thing does not lose its character for being abused, and there are circumstances under which a substantial mark of public esteem may be offered and accepted with entire propriety. Such circumstances attend the proposal of a testimonial to Sir Julius Benedict on the occasion of his seventieth birthday, which will be celebrated at the end of the present month. The suggestion comes from those who are best able, by reason of many years' artistic and friendly association with this eminent musician, to estimate both the value of his services and the worth of his personal character. But no recommendation of the kind is necessary. The name and fame of Sir Julius Benedict have long been the property, so to speak, of the nation he adopted forty years ago—the nation which is proud to have him enrolled in the number of its sons; and from all parts of England will assuredly come a warm response to the proposal now made. Few men of eminence in the artistic world have such a great and general claim to that practical form of gratitude which shapes itself in deeds. As a composer, Sir Julius possesses the admiration of all—of those on the one hand whose highest tastes are gratified by a simple song like "Rock me to sleep;" of those, on the other, who can appreciate lofty works of art, such as the Symphony No. 1 and the Oratorio of *St. Peter*. Between these extremes lies a wide space, the whole of which Sir Julius Benedict has covered with successes given to very few. Need we say that one who has done such things for the most universal of arts is a benefactor whose worth deserves acknowledgment? What Sir Julius Benedict has been in the study he has been at the conductor's desk, and on the concert platform—always devoting a commanding talent, with unflagging zeal, to the business in hand. More than this, what the eminent composer has been to art, he has been to artists, many of whom are able to speak gratefully of wise council and active help, given in the midst of arduous labours with a readiness which has doubled the value of the gift. Let all these things be remembered, and the veteran master, who so soon will look back upon threescore years and ten, may anticipate a tribute to the value of his services such as will not only crown his career with rejoicing, but impress upon his younger colleagues the fact that the highest honours belong to him who with natural gifts combines unwearied industry and the virtues of a blameless life.

(From the " Graphic.")

It is proposed to offer to Sir Julius Benedict, on the occasion of the seventieth anniversary of his birthday, which falls on the 27th inst., a testimonial expressive of the high esteem he has won during a residence of about forty years in this country, and in appreciation of the services he has rendered to musical art, both through his genius as a composer and his steady adherence to what is right and good for the profession of which he has long been one of the most sterling representatives. No proposition of the kind could, we feel assured, be hailed with more unanimous satisfaction.

INTRODUCTION and POLONAISE BRILLANTE,
Op. 3, for Pianoforte and Violoncello. *Chopin.*

(First performance at the Popular Concerts.)

Introduzione, Lento; leading to
Allegro con spirito alla Polacca—C major.

Dr. HANS VON BÜLOW and Signor PEZZE.

From this very early work of the afterwards celebrated
Chopin (" Chopinetto," as Mendelssohn used playfully to call
him*) a simple quotation or so from each movement will
suffice.

The *Introduzione* begins with a short prelude for pianoforte alone :—

* See the interesting and admirable little volume—*Mendelssohn,
Letters and Recollections,* written by Dr. Ferdinand Hiller, and,
with his consent and kind revision, translated by M. E. Von Glehn.
(Macmillan and Co.)

upon which follows the subjoined melody for the violoncello :—

—the pianoforte accompanying it as below :—

This movement does not come to a full close, but, breaking off on the dominant, through a brilliant *cadenza*, which may speak for itself, leads to the theme of the Polacca :—

Further on there is a counter theme for the violoncello, in the key of F major :—

From the eighth bar (☞) this is joined by a brilliant pianoforte accompaniment, after the subjoined pattern :—

It is unnecessary to cite any additional examples from this simply planned, though showy, piece.

Chopin produced in all about seventy works—including two grand concertos for piano with orchestral accompaniments, two grand sonatas for piano solo, a sonata for pianoforte and violoncello, other pieces with orchestral accompaniments, several books of studies and preludes, together with a large number of *nocturnes, polonaises, ballades,* scherzos, mazurkas, variations, &c. These do not include his posthumous works, two volumes of which have appeared—the last consisting of *sixteen Polish Songs,* numbered Op. 47 (why it is difficult to say, "Op. 47" being affixed to his *Troisième Ballade,* in A flat), and published some years ago, with the original Polish words, and German versions by Herr Gumbert, the popular lyric poet. That Chopin, however, excelled less in works of "*longue haleine*" than in those of smaller pretensions, will hardly be denied. His *Etudes,* his *Preludes,* his *Valses,* his *Nocturnes,*

and above all, his Mazurkas, are quite enough to save him
from oblivion, whatever may eventually become of his concertos
and sonatas. The varied manner in which he has said
the same thing some fifty times over will go further than
anything else to prove that Chopin's talent, whatever its eccen-
tricities and failings, was decidedly inventive. The best of the
Mazurkas are without question those that smell least strongly of
the lamp; those which, harmonized in the least affected manner,
are easiest to play, and bear the closest affinity to (in some cases
are almost echoes of) the national dance tunes of his country.
Many of them are gems, as faultless as they are attractive,
from whatever point of view regarded; others, more evidently
laboured, are less happy; but not one is wholly destitute
of points that appeal to the feelings, surprise by their unex-
pectedness, fascinate by their plaintive character, or charm by
their ingenuity.*

Frederick Chopin was born in 1810, at Zelazowa-Wola,
near Warsaw, and died in Paris on the 17th of October, 1849,
He was buried in the cemetery of Père la Chaise, between
the tombs of Bellini and Cherubini. His obsequies were
celebrated with great pomp at the Madeleine, Mozart's
Requiem forming part of the service, in accordance with a
desire which Chopin had often expressed.

---

* The Mazurkas of Frederick Chopin, edited by J. W. Davison.

NEW SONG, Miss ANTOINETTE STERLING.

Music by Arthur Sullivan.

Words by ADELAIDE PROCTOR.

"THOU ART WEARY."

Hush! I cannot bear to see thee
  Stretch thy tiny hands in vain;
Dear, I have no bread to give thee—
  Nothing, child, to ease thy pain.
When God sent thee first to bless me,
  Proud and thankful too was I;
Now, my darling, I—thy mother—
  Almost long to see thee die.
Sleep, my darling, thou art weary;
God is good, but life is dreary.

Better thou shouldst perish early,
  Starve so soon, my darling one,
Than in helpless sin and sorrow
  Vainly live—as I have done!
Better that thy angel spirit
  With my joy, my peace were flown,
Than thy heart grow cold and careless,
  Reckless, hopeless—like my own!
Sleep, my darling, thou art weary;
God is good, but life is dreary.

I am wasted, dear, with hunger,
  And my brain is all opprest;
I have scarcely strength to press thee,
  Wan and feeble, to my breast.
Patience, baby, God will help us:
  Death will come to thee and me;
He will take us to his Heaven,
  Where no want or pain can be.
Sleep, my darling, thou art weary;
God is good, but life is dreary.

---

* Published by CHAPPELL and Co. 50, New Bond Street.

QUINTET, in D minor, Op. 130, for Pianoforte, two Violins, Viola, and Violoncello. *Spohr.*

(First performance at the Popular Concerts.)

Allegro moderato—D minor and major.
Scherzo, moderato—D minor; with
Trio—B flat major.
Adagio assai—A major.
Finale (vivace)—D major.

Dr. HANS VON BÜLOW, M. SAINTON,

Herr L. RIES, Mr. ZERBINI, and Signor PEZZE.

To-day's analytical programme is already so long that it is impossible to do more than hint at the leading themes of the four movements into which this quintet is divided. The plan, however, like that of nearly all Spohr's compositions for the chamber, is, after the long accepted orthodox model, clear, symmetrical, and easily followed out.

Allegro moderato (first theme).

(Second theme—pianoforte and violoncello parts only.)

Scherzo (theme).

Violins.

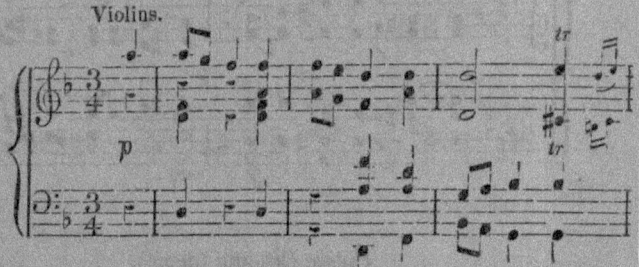

Pianoforte.

Trio.

Adagio (theme).

Pianoforte.

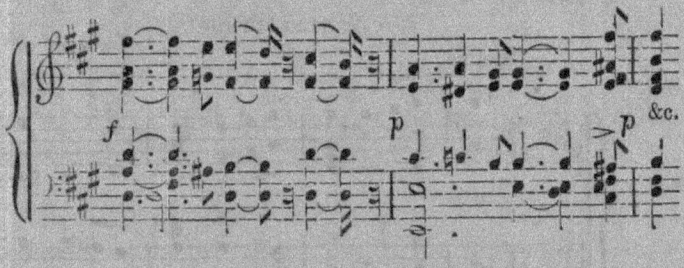

Finale (leading theme).

(Second theme—A major.)

1st Violin and Cello in octaves.

A casual reference is made to this quintet in the second part of Spohr's *Selbst-Biographie;* but all that can be gathered is that it was composed some time in the autumn of 1845, shortly after the 15th violin concerto and the quintet for stringed instruments (both in E minor), and shortly before the 30th stringed quartet and the quartet-concertante. The opera of the *Kreuzfahrer* ("Crusaders") was played at Berlin early in the same year—the year, by the way, of the Festival at Bonn, to celebrate the uncovering of Beethoven's statue, at which Spohr was present, to conduct the Mass in D and the Ninth Symphony.

———

END OF THE FOUR HUNDRED AND EIGHTY-SEVENTH
CONCERT.

———

J. MALLETT, PRINTER, 59, WARDOUR STREET, SOHO. W.

MONDAY POPULAR CONCERTS.

MONDAY EVENING, NOVEMBER 16th, 1874.

PROGRAMME.

PART I.

QUARTET, in A minor, Op. 41, No. 1, for two Violins, Viola, and Violoncello...*Schumann.*

MM. STRAUS, L. RIES, ZERBINI, and PIATTI.

SONG, " L'ombrosa notte vien." ....*Hummel.*

Madlle. NITA GAËTANO.

SUITE, in D minor, for Pianoforte alone........ ....*Handel.*

Dr. HANS VON BÜLOW.

PART II.

TRIO, in A minor, Op. 124, for Pianoforte, Violin, and Violoncello ....*Spohr.*

(First time at the Popular Concerts.)

MM. HANS VON BÜLOW, STRAUS, and PIATTI.

SONGS, { " A flow'ret thou resemblest." } ....*Schumann.*
{ " A Spring Night." }

Madlle. NITA GAËTANO.

SONATA, in F major, Op. 5, No. 1, for Pianoforte and Violoncello ....*Beethoven.*

MM. HANS VON BÜLOW and PIATTI.

Conductor   -   -   Mr. ZERBINI.

O.

www.ingramcontent.com/pod-product-compliance
Lightning Source LLC
Chambersburg PA
CBHW082052220626
47052CB00006B/1214